TAKE AWAY

THE RED ZONE

TAKE AWAY

BRANDON TERRELL

darbycreek

MINNEAPOLIS

Darby Creek
A division of Lerner Publishing Group, Inc.
241 First Avenue North
Minneapolis, MN 55401 USA

For reading levels and more information, look up this title
at www.lernerbooks.com.

The images in this book are used with the permission of: © Mike Powell/
CORBIS, (football player); © iStockphoto.com/mack2happy (grass).

Main body text set in Janson Text LT Std 12/17.5
Typeface provided by Linotype AG.

Library of Congress Cataloging-in-Publication Data

Terrell, Brandon, 1978–
    Take away / by Brandon Terrell.
        pages   cm. — (The red zone ; #5)
    Summary: After a clash with Coach Z, the Central High Trojan's star wide receiver, Orlando Green, decides to play for the Trojan's archrival, the Athens High Raiders, leaving his best friend Devon to deal with the consequences.
    ISBN 978-1-4677-2130-1 (lib. bdg : alk. paper)
    ISBN 978-1-4677-4653-3 (eBook)
    [1. Football—Fiction. 2. High schools—Fiction. 3. Schools—Fiction. 4. Loyalty—Fiction. 5. Conduct of life—Fiction.] I. Title.
PZ7.T273Tak 2014
[Fic]—dc23   2013046624

Manufactured in the United States of America
1 – SB – 7/15/14

FOR MY TWO ALL-STARS

"Pathetic! You guys call yourselves a football team?"

Even in the dim light of the school library, where the entire Troy Central High Trojan football team sat watching game film, I could see Coach Z's face turning about ten different shades of red. Even the vein in the middle of his forehead made an appearance.

"You don't deserve a state championship,"

he continued. "Not after what I saw last Friday night."

The team sat in rows of uncomfortable metal folding chairs. I was in the back, behind a couple of massive offensive linemen, slouched low in my chair. The linemen blocked for me on the field. On footage days, they did the same off the field. Coach Z stood in front of us, hands balled into fists. Behind him was a flat-screen television on a librarian's cart. Coach had paused the game film from last Friday's loss at a crucial offensive drive late in the second quarter.

Coach Z—his last name was really Zachary, but no one ever called him that, probably not even his wife—had every right to be angry. Last Friday night, we'd lost to a team we should have beaten. At home, no less. It was embarrassing.

"Devon!"

My heart jumped as Coach Z called out my name. I didn't like to make waves, except on the field. My philosophy for life was the same as it was for football: keep your head down, keep moving forward, and do what's required of you. Right then, though, what I was required to do went against the first part. Because right then, I had to answer Coach Z.

I straightened up in my chair. "Yeah, Coach?"

"Maybe my eyes are just getting old," Coach Z said, sarcasm dripping off his words, "but it seems to me like Davis spent all game searching for a linebacker to hit and didn't find any. Am I right?"

I paused. Dylan Davis was the team's fullback. His thankless job was to block for me, the team's halfback. He didn't mind—Dylan loved knocking guys down, linebackers especially—but he'd missed some pretty crucial blocks on Friday. I didn't want to call him out, but Coach Z already knew the answer to his own question.

I nodded. "Yeah."

"Hard to score if you can't find an open seam, isn't it?"

"Yes, Coach."

Dylan shot me a glare as Coach started up the game film again. On the screen, Orlando Green, our bullet-fast wide receiver, ran a corner route. As he cut toward the back left corner of the end zone, Shane Hunter, QB1 and class-A jerk, lofted a tight spiral that danced off Orlando's fingertips and landed in the grass.

Coach Z paused the film. "There was nobody even close to you, Orlando. You could have walked into the end zone, for crying out loud. That's a routine catch, and you managed to flush six points right down the toilet."

Orlando, whose ego was about as big as the town of Troy, shook his head. "Ain't my fault, Coach," he said. "The ball sailed on me."

"Whatever, dude." Shane piped up, defending himself. "That throw was perfect. You just couldn't pull it in."

"Shane's right," Coach Z said. "Your head wasn't in the game, Green. You botched routes. Missed blocks." He jabbed a finger at the TV screen. "Dropped balls."

Orlando could be a hothead. It was only one of his many wonderful qualities. I could see his anger had nearly boiled over. He stood up, stepped toward Coach Z, and said, "I'm the best player you got on the field, and you know it." His voice echoed off the library walls. "If that ball had been catchable, I would have caught it. So don't be acting like I'm the reason we lost that game."

"Don't you talk to me like that," Coach Z said. "Sit down, you disrespectful punk."

"Why don't you make me?"

Nobody said a word. The library was so quiet, you could have heard a penalty flag drop. Which is actually pretty common for a library, come to think of it. But seeing Orlando and Coach Z face off like that? It was like watching two bears clawing at each other. No way was I getting in the middle.

Coach Colby, who ran the defense, was the brave soul who stepped in. "Take ten," he said, placing a hand on Orlando's chest. "Cool off. Then suit up and meet at the fifty-yard line. Got it?"

"Yeah, I got it," Orlando answered, not taking his eyes off Coach Z.

"Everybody," Colby added, "On the field in ten."

The team mumbled in acknowledgment. We hit the locker room a few minutes later, going through the almost religious routine of strapping on our pads, lacing up our cleats, and taking the field. I ran down the tunnel leading to Willard Auto Parts Field alongside Orlando. He didn't say a word. He was still fuming.

In the world of high school football, Coach Z was immortal, a titan who demanded respect. Everyone on the team—and even some of their parents—lived and died by what Coach Z said.

After warming up, we split into offense and defense. I was one of the major offensive playmakers, known around the school as the Big Six. The name didn't bug me. I tried not to pay too much attention to it. Instead, I focused on what I needed to do on the field to win.

We lined up on the twenty-yard line. Coach Z, wearing the same red-and-white hooded sweatshirt he always wore, called plays from the backfield.

"Run the corner route!"

This was the same play that had led Orlando and Coach Z toward a shouting match in the library. Shane took the snap, and I sprinted into my spot near the right guard. During the game, my job would be to pick up a block on any blitzing defender. At practice, though, I kept my eyes downfield and saw Orlando sprinting along the right sideline. He cut hard and dashed toward the middle of the field. Shane slung the ball in a high arc. It dropped right into Orlando's waiting hands.

"Good," Z said. "Run it again."

Orlando hurried back, took up his spot on the line, and broke downfield once more. Like before, he caught the pass easily.

Coach Z was not impressed. "Again."

Orlando jogged from his position thirty yards down the field back to the line.

"Hustle it up, Green!" Coach Z shouted. "Easy to make a catch like that when you don't have a safety or two buzzing around you, isn't it?"

Corner route. Spiral. Fingertip catch. Perfect.

"Again!"

My stomach turned to stone. I knew what was going on but took my place behind Shane like I always did.

Orlando, winded, caught the ball for a fourth time.

"Nice work," Coach Z said. Then he added, "Again!"

Orlando stopped ten yards from the line. I could see his chest heaving as he tried to catch his breath.

"Let's go, Green!" Coach Z said, clapping his hands. "I thought you were the best player I had on the field."

Orlando began to walk toward us, hand on his hip.

"Pick up the pace!"

"Screw this." Orlando unstrapped his helmet and peeled it off. In the cold evening air, steam swirled off his head.

"Hey! Nobody takes off their helmet on my field!" Coach Z threw his clipboard down onto the grass. "You hear me?"

Orlando turned his back on Coach Z. He walked to the sidelines, bent over a bench, and puked his lunch all over the ground.

The whole team had stopped practicing. Everyone was watching Orlando.

"I'm outta here," he said. He began to walk back toward the tunnel.

Coach Z bellowed after him, "You leave this field, you're never stepping foot on it again! You hear me?"

Orlando didn't react. He let the shadows of the tunnel swallow him.

2/MONDAY, OCTOBER 28—
DOYLE'S PIZZERIA

I'd just left the locker room and was slinging my backpack onto the passenger seat of my busted-up car when I got a text from Orlando: *MEET ME @ DOYLES.*

Doyle's was a pizza joint in the oldest neighborhood of Troy. The interior was dark, with wood-paneled walls and booths that had been around for almost fifty years. The place was also a shrine to all things Troy football. Its owner,

Wally Doyle, had played for *the Team*, the undefeated Trojans squad that included Coach Z, Coach Whitson, and a number of other men still associated with our team.

Wally Doyle was also a member of the Friends of Troy Football Board, a bunch of ex-players and dads trying to relive their glory days through their kids. The walls of Doyle's were covered in football gear, programs, and photos of every team to hit the field at Troy Central High, from the 1950s to the photo of our squad taken at the start of this season.

Wally stood at the front counter. He was a tall man with a shock of silver hair. He spied me the minute I walked into the place.

"Well, if it ain't the fastest halfback in Ohio," he said, a wide grin on his weathered face.

"Hey, Wally," I said. "Orlando here?"

"Indeed he is. The usual spot." Wally reached behind the counter and snatched a giant plastic cup. "Fill her up. And of course, pizza's on me tonight, Devon."

I hit the fountain soda and filled the cup with a mixture of every flavor. A suicide, we called it.

Then I found Orlando sitting alone at a booth in the back. He was sipping from a matching monster cup, his head craned toward the TV mounted on the wall. *Monday Night Football* was about to start, the Cowboys taking on the Bears at Soldier Field.

"Hey, Orlando," I said.

"'Sup."

I slid into the booth across from him and shed my coat. We didn't say anything for a bit, just stared at the broadcasters on TV breaking down yesterday's NFL games. Doyle's wasn't too crowded, making it easy enough to hear the small TV.

I always felt a little strange eating at the place. All of the Troy memorabilia. All of the history. My family and I moved to town a couple years back, when my dad got a job at the soybean plant outside of Troy, so I haven't always bled Trojan red and white. Unlike the rest of the team.

Right around kickoff, Wally dropped by our booth with a basket of garlic bread and a large supreme with extra veggies. "Gotta keep you boys fed and ready to play," Wally said. "Tough loss on Friday. Lot of missed plays and dropped balls, but that's easy to correct, am I right?"

Orlando held his tongue.

"Thanks, Wally," I said.

We noshed on pizza and watched as the Bears drove the length of the field and stalled in the red zone. As they lined up to kick a field goal, Orlando tossed his slice of pizza down and said, "I'm done, man."

"Dude, we still got half a pizza," I said, taking a huge bite. A strand of cheese hung down my chin.

Orlando shook his head. "Not what I mean, D. I'm done with Coach Z. With Troy football. I can't take it anymore. Not after today."

I laughed. "Whatever. You had a bad practice. Get over it."

"Nah, man. Don't you see it? Coach Z? He don't care about us. He just wants another trophy in the case, and he don't care how he gets it."

"Yeah, that's the point. Trophies. Championships. Legacies. Look around, man." I waved a hand at the red-and-white-cluttered walls of Doyle's. "That's what this town is all about."

"Not me," Orlando said. "Yeah, I wanna win. But I want respect. I've got more skills in one pinkie than Z ever had in his whole body. He wants to win, he's gonna need me."

"What are you saying, Orlando? That you're just gonna quit the team? With two games left? Dude, if we want to even *make* the play-offs, we have to win both games. You're willing to just . . . give up on us?"

"I don't know."

"Don't be stupid."

Orlando kept his eyes on the television. I couldn't believe it. Yeah, Orlando thought pretty big about himself, but he had the talent to back it up. He really was the best player on the field. He danced around defensive secondaries and held a couple of school records, including most receiving touchdowns in Troy Central High history. Losing him this close to a state championship run would be devastating.

After a few moments of awkward silence, Orlando slipped out of the booth. "I'll catch you later, Devon," he said.

He wove his way between booths and tables, stopping when he reached the massive vintage photo of *the Team* on the wall near the door, where everyone who entered Doyle's was sure to see it. Orlando flipped off the photo's young, smiling Coach Z. Then he shouldered open the door and left me with half a pizza and a bunch of questions.

3/TUESDAY, OCTOBER 29—
TROY CENTRAL HIGH SCHOOL

Coach Whitson always unlocked the outside door to the locker room at 6 a.m. And I was always there at 6:01 to hit the weight room before school. It felt good to get my reps in before class. I liked to drive myself to the limit and loved the sensation of burning muscles. It woke me up far better than a jolt of morning caffeine.

Usually, Orlando was there with me, blasting hip-hop from the stereo at a volume high enough to rattle the walls. The morning after our talk, though, I'd had a sinking feeling that he was going to be a no-show, and I was right. The only players joining me in the weight room that morning were Brian Norwood and a couple of defensive linemen.

Brian spotted for me while I did my reps on the bench press. On the ceiling above me, in letters made of black tape, were the words *PUSH YOURSELF*. Orlando had been the one to add that bit of motivation for the team at the beginning of conditioning, way back in June.

Sweat stung my eyes, making my vision blur. My arms quaked as I pushed up the last rep and locked the bar back onto the bench. I sat up and wiped my face with a towel.

How could Orlando just abandon me—abandon the *whole team*—this way? It was selfish, which, in all honesty, meant it was a pretty Orlando thing to do.

The first bell was about to ring, and I had to hit my locker before getting to class. I ate a couple of energy bars as I walked. Breakfast of champions.

As I rounded a corner, I almost ran right into Shane. He was walking with a couple of the guys—our left guard, Truman, and Terry Foster, who had once played for our rivals, the Evil Empire of Athens High. Shane smiled ear to ear when he saw me.

"Hey, Shaw, where's your boyfriend this morning?" he asked.

"No clue, Hunter," I mumbled. I wasn't in the mood to take Shane's garbage.

"Nice little hissy fit he threw on the field yesterday."

"Lay off," I said, defending Orlando. "It was one dropped pass. Coach Z didn't have to be so hard on him."

"That was nothing," Shane said. "Green's lucky he's Big Six. Otherwise, he'd be watching the game from the sidelines after a tantrum like that."

The first bell echoed through the hall. Kids around us hustled to get to class before the second bell made them tardy. I lowered my head and brushed past Shane.

"See ya, Shaw," he said. "And if you talk to Green, tell him it's okay if he wants to bring his pacifier to practice."

Shane and the other dudes laughed. I just walked away.

Orlando and I didn't have class together until third period, Coach Whitson's easy-A business class. I found my desk near the back and glanced over to where Orlando should be sitting. Empty. Crap.

Shane and a couple of the other guys sat up front, and they didn't seem to notice—or care—that Orlando was absent. I'd hoped that this morning was just a fluke, that our conversation at Doyle's was nothing to worry about, and that he'd still be in class. Knowing Orlando hadn't been at school all morning was twisting my stomach into knots.

I sent him a quick text: *WHERE R U?*. Then I crammed my phone back into my pocket before Coach Whitson saw it and confiscated it.

I spent the rest of the day hoping that Orlando hadn't done anything rash or stupid. As I walked into the locker room after classes to suit up for practice, my phone buzzed in my pocket. My fears were officially justified.

Orlando had sent me a message.

It read: *NEW COLORS YO!*

Below the words was a photo of Orlando wearing the red and black of the Athens Raiders.

My phone felt like a ticking time bomb. I hadn't shown anyone the photo from Orlando, and at Monday's practice I'd stuffed the phone inside my backpack where no one could snatch it. I'd done the same thing the next morning.

The team was starting to ask questions. *Is Orlando sick? Is he pouting? Will he be back in time for Friday's game against Bradbury?* But so far, no one knew the terrible truth.

Except me.

The early evening air had a bite to it. I sat high up in the bleachers at Athens High School. Enemy territory. I had the hood of my gray sweatshirt pulled up, the bill of my Bengals cap pulled low. No way was I going to let one of the Raiders players identify me.

I'd left practice a bit early by telling Coach Z I felt nauseous. It wasn't far from the truth. The whole drive from Troy to Athens, I'd kept the window down for fear I'd puke in the car.

I'd prayed that Orlando's text had been a joke or maybe a look at an early Halloween costume. But he was out there on the field, wearing a red-and-black uniform, number 89. The Raiders were running offensive drills.

I watched as he ran a cross pattern, caught the ball, and broke for the sideline. The coach blew the whistle and slapped Orlando on the helmet while barking, "Nice catch!"

Orlando high-fived the Raiders' starting quarterback, a kid named Jack Wayne.

As practice continued, I started to recognize a couple of plays, especially ones that featured the halfback. They ran a twenty-two red dog, a power option sweep that looked almost exactly like the one we ran. Their defense lined up in a pressure D, with eight guys near the line of scrimmage, as the offense tried to power the ball up the gut in a play Coach Z called a ninety-nine gold.

It was almost like the Raiders were working out of our playbook. Like they were trying to determine the best defensive formation against the Trojan running game.

Orlando and Jack Wayne jogged over to the sidelines, where the Raiders head coach stood with his clipboard. The trio discussed something, and I saw Orlando point down at the clipboard, as if he were doing the coaching.

When they hit the field again, the Raider offense practiced running a double reverse. Jack Wayne pitched the ball to their halfback, who flipped the ball into Orlando's hands. Orlando ran wide around the corner, sweeping to the sideline. Coach Z had a trick play nearly identical to it in the Trojan book, but we rarely used it.

And then it hit me like a helmet to the gut: the Raiders didn't just *look* like they were using our playbook. They were actually *using our playbook.*

What was Orlando thinking?

When practice was over and the Raiders had jogged off the field, I left the bleachers and waited in the parking lot. The sun had gone down, leaving the parking lot blanketed in deep shadows. I found Orlando's car and leaned against the side.

He came out about fifteen minutes later, laughing about something with three other players. It was like he'd been a part of the team for more than, oh, I don't know, *one stupid practice.* They split up when they hit the parking lot, high-fiving each other before heading off to their own cars.

Orlando didn't see me until he was almost to his vehicle. He jumped back, surprised. When I dropped my hood, he relaxed. "D, you're gonna give me a heart attack," he laughed, punching me lightly on the shoulder. "I thought maybe you was somebody looking for a wallet to swipe."

I was in no mood to joke around. "Orlando, what are you doing?"

"Oh come on, man," Orlando said, rolling his eyes. "Not this again."

"How can you betray us like this?" I asked. "And with *Athens*?"

"Yeah, I bet Coach Z flipped when he found out, am I right?"

I shook my head. "He doesn't know yet."

"For real? 'Cause I can't wait to hear what he does when you tell him." Orlando dug out his car keys, unlocking the driver's side door and tossing his equipment bag across to the passenger seat. "You want to get something to eat?"

I shook my head.

"Cool. See ya, D."

Orlando started to climb into the car. I grabbed the doorframe and stopped him. "Those were our plays, weren't they?" I asked. "*Trojan* plays. Don't tell me you gave these guys our playbook. If we have to face them again in the play-offs, they'll know our every move. How stupid could you be, dude?" I wasn't normally confrontational—the opposite, in fact—and

Orlando knew it. I could see in his eyes that I was freaking him out a little.

"They're just plays, man," Orlando said, shaking his head. "It's not like Coach Z invented them."

"So you aren't denying it?"

"Devon, you know how they say, 'The grass is always greener'?" Orlando asked. "Well, over here, they respect me. They understand my talent and don't drag me down for dropped catches and missed blocks. Over here? The grass is seriously green. You should think about seeing it for yourself."

I released my death grip on the door, and Orlando swung it closed. He fired up the car, waved through the closed window, and peeled out of the dark parking lot, leaving me all alone again.

Orlando was getting really good at that.

Shane knew.

He walked down the hall toward me, his fists clenched at his sides, his jaw locked tight. I had been making my way to history class, but all the sudden, I felt like *I* was going to be history.

I tried to act calm. Maybe I was wrong. Maybe Shane's latest girlfriend just found out he was only an overachiever on the football field. "'Sup, QB1?"

Shane grabbed me by the shirt with both hands and slammed me against the lockers. A handle jabbed me in the small of my back.

Yep. Shane knew.

"When were you going to tell us, Shaw?" he asked. Tiny flecks of spit shot out from between his teeth. Gross. "Orlando's playing for the Raiders now?"

I pushed Shane back until I was clear of the locker. He released his grip. Around us, people had stopped to stare. The team was supposed to be a unit. Nobody needed to see us acting like a bunch of fools.

"Stop," I said. "This isn't the place."

"Why didn't you tell us?" Shane's voice had dropped to almost a whisper. "We're your team. You're *Big Six*." He shook his head. "Big mistake, Shaw."

"Is there a problem here?" Mrs. Norwood, my language arts teacher, approached us. She carried a coffee mug in one hand and a stack of papers in the other. Like usual, she had a no-nonsense look on her face. She was one of the few who didn't put up with all our football extracurriculars.

Shane flashed her a big QB1 smile anyway. "Not at all, Mrs. Norwood," he said. "Just a couple of Big Sixers goofing around is all."

Mrs. Norwood didn't look very convinced. "Stop horsing around and get to class, boys," she said.

Shane tossed a last, long glare at me, then walked away as if nothing had happened.

After school, while gearing up for practice in the locker room, nobody said a word to me. Not even Brian Norwood, who usually slapped my shoulder pads to amp me up. I jogged down the tunnel alone, helmet in hand.

Coach Z stood on the sidelines, his arms crossed on his chest. The rest of the team knelt in a semicircle around Coach Whitson in the middle of the field. I took a knee behind Terry and Truman as Z stepped up to the team.

I expected Coach Z to be furious. I expected swearing, yelling, spitting, thunderclouds clapping, and lightning overhead. What I *didn't* expect was for him to be . . . *calm*.

"It's simple," he said. "Winners never quit, and quitters never win. I'll give you one guess who said that." We all knew. Coach Z had a tendency to quote Vince Lombardi every chance he got. "You all heard the news, no doubt. Orlando Green is gone. Defected to Athens. His ego is their problem now."

Coach Z's gaze met mine. Even though he didn't seem angry, I still felt a chill down my back.

"Our focus is on tomorrow," Z continued. "Not on last Friday. Not on Benedict Green. No, the only thing that matters now is beating the Cyclones on their home turf. We persevere, because *we are winners!*"

The team let out a mighty cheer.

We ran sprints up and down the field, the dirt and grass grinding between our cleats. My lungs burned, and it felt good to worry about something other than Orlando for a while.

The team split into offense and defense, and we spent a good deal of time running plays. Right away, Shane, in his red mesh quarterback's jersey, called for the draw play. He hesitated before handing me the ball, giving the line time to open a gap. Then he shoved the ball into my gut so hard, I coughed out my mouth guard.

Yep. Shane was still mad.

He wasn't the only one. Toward the end of practice, we usually have a little scrimmage. There typically isn't much tackling, for obvious reasons. We don't need one of our starters to get hurt because of a silly scrimmage. During that day's scrimmage, though, whenever I got the ball, the defense took me down. Hard. And Coach Z let them. I understood why. They were upset at Orlando, and he wasn't around. So they needed someone else to hit.

And I was their punching bag.

When Shane checked down on a pass play and threw me the ball in the flat, the linebackers read it, and Norwood came at me low, smashing into my waist with his shoulders and knocking me to the ground. The ball fell from my hand and landed beside me. Like sharks attacking chum, the defense dove at it. I wound up at the bottom of a pile, fingers clawing at my helmet.

My left hand was bent and pinned under me. I could feel pain shooting up my arm like pinpricks. But I couldn't get up.

Coach Z's whistle pierced the air, and the defense slowly pried themselves off one another. Brian came up with the ball, and the others patted him on the back. I was the last man on the ground.

Nobody helped me up. I wiggled the fingers of my left hand, rotating my wrist back and forth. It hurt like hell—was going to bruise for sure—but I gritted my teeth.

"You all right, Shaw?" Coach Z asked.

I nodded. "Tweaked my wrist a bit."

"Shake it off," Z said. "Line up. Run it again."

6/FRIDAY, NOVEMBER 1—
TROY CENTRAL HIGH PEP RALLY

Every Friday during football season, the students and faculty of Troy Central High cram into the gymnasium bleachers for a pep rally instead of going to eighth period. The school band plays a few songs, including the Trojan fight song. The cheerleaders stand at the middle of the gym floor and perform a routine full of flips, high kicks, and shaking pom-poms. There's even a section of chairs set up near the door for parents who took off work to join in the festivities, a section that's always overflowing. And the football team sits together on a platform under one of the raised basketball hoops. It's a thundering display of school pride.

We were just an hour or so from packing up and busing to Bradbury to take on the Cyclones. I sat in my usual spot—back row, hunched in my chair—massaging my bruised and swollen left wrist. It had kept me up the night before, chewing aspirin. My room got to smelling like Icy Hot. But I wasn't going to say anything, not even to our trainer. Instead, I kept popping aspirin every couple of hours and wrapped it tight.

The band finished belting out a loud rendition of "We Will Rock You." After the packed bleachers full of screaming students trailed off, Coach Z stepped up to a microphone stand.

"Students of Troy High," he said, his commanding voice echoing off the gymnasium walls, "Are you ready to watch your football team kick some Cyclone butt tonight?"

Another roar. The gym rumbled like a low-grade earthquake as all the people in the bleachers stomped their feet.

Coach Z held up a hand, and just like that, the sound ceased. "Thought so. Now, how about we hear a few words from your captain, Shane Hunter!"

Shane stood up in his front-row seat as the crowd screeched. He took the microphone from Coach Z, who draped his arm around Shane's shoulder all buddy-buddy.

"Thanks, Coach," Shane said. "So . . . we've had a tough week. We not only lost a game but also an important member of our team." A chorus of boos filled the gym. I heard one kid in the back of the bleachers shout, "Orlando sucks!"

Shane lowered the mic and turned briefly away from the crowd, toward the team. I could have sworn I saw a smile flicker across his face.

He spoke once more to his adoring fans. "I've got a question for you. Who here wants to go show Bradbury High what a championship football team looks like?!"

I didn't think the cheers in the gymnasium could get any louder than they already were.

I was wrong.

By the time we'd gathered our things in the locker room and headed out to the bus, the crowd from the gym had migrated to the parking lot. They parted like the Red Sea as the team exited the locker room, led by Shane and Coach Z.

We rode to away games on a red-and-white coach bus. The fine folks on the Friends of Troy Football Board had paid for the custom paint job. Our bus was parked at the front of a line of other buses. The rest would caravan behind us, packed to the brim with our schoolmates. It didn't matter how far away the game was. Trojan football fans filled the stands at every game. Coach Z always said, "There's a reason they build bleachers on both sides of the field, and it isn't so that one side stays empty."

I was one of the last players on the bus. The rest of the guys sat or stood in the back, laughing and joking. Terry was doing an impression of Orlando that made my stomach turn. It was like they didn't remember he was their friend and teammate less than a week ago.

I didn't want anything to do with them. So I slid into a seat toward the front, just behind the coaches, who were already going over the game plan.

It was weird. For the first time since becoming a Trojan, I no longer felt like I was a part of the team. Even as one of the Big Six, I'd become an outsider. I thought back to what Orlando had said, about how green the grass was over at Athens.

Funny. I was starting to understand what he meant.

7/FRIDAY, NOVEMBER 1— AWAY GAME AGAINST THE BRADBURY CYCLONES

Bradbury High sat on the outskirts of the town, surrounded by fields and open space and pretty much nothing else. Even though it was a fairly new building, the campus looked like a prison. There was nothing to block the wind and cold, and there were plenty of both by the time we took the field. A light drizzle started to fall.

I stood on the sidelines, watching my breath

cloud in front of my helmet and rubbing my gloved hands together. The cold weather and adrenaline at least made the pain in my wrist disappear for a while.

The Cyclones won the coin toss and deferred, so we got the ball first. With Orlando gone, Dylan Davis had taken over his spot on special teams. He took the kickoff, found a seam, and ran straight through the Bradbury defenders until he was tripped up around the forty-yard line.

Nearby, Shane shouted, "Let's go, offense!" He shoved his helmet on, slapped Dylan's pads, and jogged onto the field. I followed.

The rain started to come down harder, which made things tougher on our passing game. That and the fact that Shane didn't have his number one receiving target anymore. So we ran the ball. The first time Shane stuffed a handoff into my arms, it felt like he was giving me a cinder block. I drove forward for about seven yards before Bradbury defenders dragged me to the ground, which may as well have been a cement slab.

We worked our way down the field, chewing up both yardage and the clock. When we reached the five-yard line, Shane called for the ninety-nine-gold. He dropped back and slid the ball into my cradled arms. I lowered my head and plowed through a hole in the right side of the Bradbury line.

I felt my hand tweak, and suddenly, I couldn't keep a grip on the ball. It tumbled to the wet, muddy grass. I twisted and spun, trying to spot it. The ball skidded across the field—right before a Bradbury player swallowed it up.

"Fumble, Trojans," the announcer said as I walked back to the sidelines, cursing under my breath. "First down, Cyclones."

"Way to go, Shaw," Shane barked at me.

"Knock it off, Hunter!" Coach Z said. "Keep your head in the game and pray your defense can hold these yahoos to a three and out."

They didn't, though. The Cyclones quarterback—a lanky kid named Jamieson—had a great arm and a fast set of legs. He moved the chains in a quick, effective way. When the Cyclones were at the fifteen, Jamieson called a QB keeper and took the ball into the end zone untouched.

Getting a W was going to be harder than we thought.

Umbrellas, blankets, and raincoats started to populate the stands. Each raindrop felt like a needle jabbing into my skin. The cold, held off by adrenaline when the game started, was creeping in and weighing us down.

On our second drive, Coach Z only called my number a couple of times. Punishment for coughing up the ball. Our backup fullback Ian, a tank on two legs, handled most of the carries. Shane passed the ball a few times, as well, but it was clear to both us *and* to Bradbury that without Orlando, our passing game was weak. Bradbury overloaded the D-line, sometimes putting as many as eight players in the box, doing everything they could to stop our running game in its tracks.

Troy was only able to push the ball past the chalk once during the entire first half, a slant pattern pass in the middle of the field to Brian that gouged through their zone defense. When the buzzer sounded at halftime, the scoreboard read: *CYCLONES: 17 TROJANS: 7.*

In the locker room at half, we sat on the wooden benches. Dripping. Coughing. Thawing.

"Winning is a habit," Coach Z said, quoting Lombardi. He paced down the line of us like a general rallying his troops. "And so is *losing*. We look sloppy out there. And it's not just because of the weather. We lack confidence. I don't know what's gotten into your heads, but in order to succeed, you need to push past it. Dig deep. Be better than them. *Be. Winners!*" He ended by banging his fist loudly on the metal lockers.

The rain let up in the second half, and our play got stronger. The Troy defense kept Jamieson and his offense out of the end zone. Shane, on the other hand, capped off a twelve-play drive by hitting Brian in the corner of the end zone. Coach Z lined us up for a two-point conversion, and Ian pounded the ball in.

Late in the fourth, we were still down by two. Our defense forced the Cyclones to punt, and Dylan ran the kick past midfield. With less than a minute left on the clock, we were going to have to pass the ball.

Shane snuck the ball past the cornerback guarding Brian, right into our tight end's hands. Brian raced up the field and darted out of bounds at the thirty-yard line.

"Same play," Shane called in the huddle. "We've only got one time-out left, and we're still out of field goal range. Whatever you do, try to get out of bounds."

Shane dropped back to pass. I did my part, laying a block on a blitzing linebacker before rolling out into the flat. The Cyclones covered Brian well this time, and they forced Shane to checkdown. He tossed the ball out to me, and I raced to the edge. I was inside the twenty-five, heading for the sidelines. One of the Cyclone safeties barreled toward me, and I switched the ball from my right hand to my left out of instinct.

Bad move.

My hand couldn't get a grip, and the ball fell loose again.

"Fumble!" I heard the safety yell.

I saw the ball at my feet, dove down, and wrapped it up. There was no way anyone was prying it loose. The safety landed hard on me, knocking the wind from my lungs.

"Time-out!" I heard Shane cry. My near-turnover had cost us valuable time and yardage, and we were forced to stop the clock instead of running another play. I twisted my head up and searched for the glowing scoreboard. The clock had stopped with five ticks left in the game.

"Field goal unit!" Coach Z waved wildly, sending our kicker, Scott, out onto the field. From where the refs had placed the ball, we were looking at a thirty-four-yard field goal. Not unheard of but still tough to manage in this kind of weather.

I knelt on the sidelines, helmet in front of me, head lowered. I couldn't watch.

I heard the snap, the kick . . .

And the Troy sideline went nuts.

I looked up in time to see the refs lift both arms to the black sky. The field goal was good. We'd won by a point, eighteen to seventeen.

Relief washed over me. It was a messy, ugly game, but we were back in the win column. That was all that mattered. I joined the rest of the team out on the field to celebrate, but nobody offered me a high five or fist bump. As Shane passed me, his shoulder pad clipped me hard, and I nearly fell to the wet ground.

Apparently, winning wasn't the only thing that mattered after all.

8/SATURDAY, NOVEMBER 2—
SHAW HOME

"Do you plan on sitting on your butt all day or what?"

My dad stood in the doorway to my room, wiping his hands on a towel, grease and oil staining his faded shirt. Every weekend, he spent time in the garage, restoring a baby blue 1965 Mustang he'd bought at an auction last summer. He was currently in the middle of rebuilding the engine, hence the black smudges on his ball cap and hands.

"Maybe," I mumbled in response.

I had been lying in bed all morning, depressed about last night's two fumbles and my injured hand. The only time I'd snuck out of my room was to steal a box of Golden Grahams and a soda from the fridge. A small TV on my desk was turned to college football, and I had every intention of watching it until the sun went down.

"Come on, Devon," Dad said, "I could use a little help."

I sighed. "Sure. Gimme a minute."

A minute turned out to be about a half hour, but eventually, I changed out of my pajamas and into a pair of old jeans and a sweatshirt. Dad was in the garage. He had the hood of the Mustang up and was bent over, examining the engine closely. A small light hung from the ceiling above it. A radio resting on the tool bench by the wall was tuned to a classic rock station.

"Hand me the socket wrench, will ya?" Dad asked, blindly reaching back for it.

I found it on the bench and passed it off with my right hand.

We worked like this for a while, Dad asking for tools like a surgeon in an operating room and me passing them off like a dutiful nurse. Finally, Dad said, "Tough game last night. I bet you were glad to get out of there with a win."

"Yeah," I said. "Can't believe I fumbled twice, though."

"Is your hand all right?" Dad knew I'd done something to it at practice the other day, but he wasn't aware of how much it was actually bugging me.

"It'll be fine."

"Just take care of yourself. Football's not worth ruining your hand, kid." Dad was a rarity here in Troy. He couldn't care less about the tradition of Trojan football. He hadn't played ball back in high school. He wasn't a member of the Friends of Troy boy's club. He didn't bow to the almighty Coach Z. He cared about his family, his faith, and his Mustang. And I loved him for it.

"Pretty strange to see Orlando miss a game like that," Dad continued. "Is he all right?"

Aside from defecting to the Evil Empire? I

thought. Most of the parents, my dad included, didn't know about Orlando's bold move. At least, not if they hadn't read today's paper. The sports section had a write-up about Athens beating the Granville Huskies at home, with Orlando catching two TD passes. At our house, I had snatched it from the kitchen counter earlier that morning.

"I'm sure he's fine," I answered. My phone began to chirp in my pocket. I dug it out, and on the screen was a text from Orlando. "Speak of the devil," I muttered.

HALLOWEEN PARTY 2NIGHT, the text read. *U IN?*

I didn't really want to go anywhere. USC was playing Ohio State, so I had a date with my television set.

NAH, SORRY MAN, I wrote back.

It didn't take long for Orlando to respond. *COME ON. GOT SOME GUYS 2 INTRO-DUCE U 2.*

RAIDER PARTY? No way I was going into enemy territory again. Shane and the guys already hated my guts. If they found out I was getting chummy with the enemy, it would be game over for me at Troy.

YUP. PICKING U UP IN 45, Orlando texted.

NO.

YES.

NO.

WEAR A COSTUME. SOMETHING THAT AIN'T RED & WHITE.

UGH. WHATEVER.

Well, it was just a little party. It's not like any of my teammates had checked in on me, seeing if I wanted to hang out with them or anything.

I shoved my phone back into my pocket. "Dad, is it cool if I go hang with Orlando for a while tonight?"

"As long as you take a shower," Dad said. "You smell like a dirty sock."

I gave him a light shove. "This coming from the man with motor oil in his hair."

"That's just my new hair product." Dad shoved me back, laughing. "Now go, get on out of here. You're no use to me here." As I started to leave, he added, "Hey, Devon?" I turned.

"Forget about last night's game, kid. It's not worth worrying over, okay?"

"Okay. Thanks, Dad." His advice was solid. I just wished he wasn't the only person in the entire town of Troy who felt that way.

9/SATURDAY, NOVEMBER 2—RAIDERS HALLOWEEN PARTY

Orlando drove me to a house outside of Athens, in the middle of Nowheresville. We turned off the highway, heading down a winding gravel road. How Orlando knew where we were going was beyond me. The house was surrounded by trees and had a huge yard. Even though Halloween had happened a couple days earlier, jack-o'-lanterns still decorated the house's front yard. A lumpy scarecrow was propped up on a wooden post and wearing a Raiders jersey. The music inside was blasting so loud, I could feel the bass pumping as we drove up.

Orlando pulled into a patch of grass on the side of the house, at the end of a line of parked cars. The party was in full force.

"So . . . whose place is this?" I asked.

Orlando shrugged. "Dunno. Some kid named Wade. He ain't on the team, but he calls himself the Raiders' biggest fan. His parents are out of town or something."

Costumed teens swarmed throughout the house. A lot of zombies covered in fake blood. Vampires. Celebrities. Even a dude in a giant pink bunny costume.

I'd brought my dad's old werewolf mask, but I was wringing it nervously in my hands instead of wearing it. Orlando and I had barely stepped through the door before someone dressed as Freddy Krueger shoved a red plastic cup into my hand. I gave it a sniff, wrinkled my nose in disgust—some sort of foul-smelling alcohol—and set it down on a nearby coffee table.

While Orlando made the rounds, flirting with every girl who made eye contact with him, I found my way to the basement. I didn't talk to anyone. Instead, I hid out in the corner of the house's game room, watching Spider-Man and Frankenstein's monster shoot a game of pool. I felt completely out of place.

Thirty minutes or so later, Orlando came down the steps, leaning in close and talking to a girl in a skimpy referee outfit. She laughed, playfully swatting his chest with one hand as if to push him away and blowing a whistle that hung around her neck.

"Illegal use of the hands," she said. "Fifteen yards!"

Orlando saw me, made his way through the crowd. "'Sup, Devon Downer?" he said. "Don't look like you're having so much fun."

"I want to bail," I told him.

He shook his head. "Nah, man. Not yet. Come on."

I followed Orlando back upstairs and out onto the patio. The backyard was huge, an acre at least, surrounded on all sides by tall trees.

The only light came from a huge bonfire. It made the shadows flicker against the trees. A bunch of teenagers huddled around it.

We walked together toward the fire, passing by a couple dressed as heavy metal rockers who'd snuck near the trees to make out. One dude sitting near the fire had a guitar, and he was trying hard to play a song that sounded vaguely familiar. A group of girls sat together, their boyfriends' letterman coats draped over their shoulders like blankets.

"Orlando, man, what's up?" I recognized the guy speaking to us: the Raiders' starting quarterback, Jack Wayne. He stood near the fire, a plastic cup in one hand. A couple more guys from the team sat next to him in old lawn chairs. None of them were dressed in costume.

"How you doin', Wayne?" Orlando and the quarterback of the Evil Empire bumped fists like it was no big deal. Then Orlando tossed his thumb back in my direction. "Y'all know Devon Shaw?"

"Hey, Devon," Jack Wayne said, stepping over and shaking my hand. The guys seated near him introduced themselves. One was Pete Burnett, the Raiders' tight end. The other guy was the team's center, Greg Grunwold. He was so massive, it looked like his lawn chair was about to give out on him.

"Nice to meet you, Devon," Jack said. "Orlando talks a lot about you."

"Huh," I said, cramming my hands in my pockets. "You mean he talks about somebody other than himself?"

The guys roared with laughter, Orlando included.

"So did he tell you about the catch he made last night?" Pete asked.

I shook my head.

"It was nuts. Double coverage, coming back at the ball—"

"I'd been flushed out of the pocket," Jack interrupted. "So I had to throw on the run."

"He tosses it up," Pete continues, "and Orlando just leaps up and pulls it in like his gloves are made out of Krazy Glue!" He leaned back in his chair, raising his arms to catch an imaginary ball. He lost his balance, toppling over backwards into the grass.

The group around the fire snickered as Pete scrambled up.

"It was sick!" Greg added, shaking his head. "I don't think I've ever seen anyone leap over two defenders like that."

"What can I say, boys?" Orlando's smile went ear to ear. I could practically see his head growing larger. "I'm a walking, talking high-light reel."

I rolled my eyes.

Jack Wayne flashed his best QB1 smile at me. It rivaled Shane Hunter's. What is it about quarterbacks? "Dude, how cool would it be if you were lining up in our backfield?"

I couldn't help myself—I laughed. "Yeah, right."

"Why not?" Orlando asked.

"Because I'm a Trojan, O," I said.

"Man, if we had Orlando *and* you, Devon," Jack said, "we'd win state for sure. Not even close."

"He's afraid of Coach Z." Orlando shook his head, disappointed. "Devon here doesn't like to

63

rock the boat, boys. Unlike this guy."

"From what Orlando's been telling us, your coach is a real jerk," Pete said.

"Yeah," Greg added. "Wouldn't you love to stick it to the guy? Beat him in the play-offs and waltz into the state championship game?"

I shrugged. The past week had been brutal. After the previous night's game, I wasn't even sure if Coach Z was going to start me next Friday, our last home game *and* our last chance to earn a spot in the play-offs. So maybe a change of scenery would be good for me. After all, these guys seemed . . . I couldn't even believe I was thinking it . . . *cool*.

"We'd be lucky to have you," Jack said. "Our back, Cody, he's good. But the way you can cut and change direction on a dime? Man, that kind of football can't be taught."

"Thanks, but you wouldn't be saying that if you saw last night's game." I rubbed my left wrist out of instinct.

"That was one game," Jack said. "A lot can change in a week."

I knew that feeling all too well.

Orlando and I stayed awhile longer, tossing logs into the bonfire and watching as the flames rose high into the sky. The cold eventually won, though. People began to trickle back inside, where the music was still playing at full volume. The bitter weather made my wrist stiff, and I told Orlando I was ready to leave.

As we walked down the gravel drive, back to Orlando's car, a dented red pickup truck roared toward the house. Its high beams were on, forcing me to shield my eyes with one arm. The truck swerved into the grass and screeched to a halt.

Two big dudes climbed out of the truck, football players in their letterman jackets. It was hard to identify them, but I was pretty sure I recognized the big lugs as D-linemen for the Raiders.

Orlando snapped off a comic salute and said, "'Sup, Ethan? Danny?"

"What are you doing here, Green?" asked the first guy. I'm pretty sure he was Ethan. His stretched letter jacket tried desperately to contain his chest. He didn't even need a costume.

Just slap him with green paint, and he could be the Incredible Hulk. "This party is for Raiders."

Orlando chuckled. "Last time I checked, I was standing in the end zone in a Raiders uni on Friday, racking up points on the scoreboard for your sorry butts."

"You may think you're God's gift to football," said the second guy, Danny. He looked like he could probably bench press two of me. "But we didn't need you to win. Still don't."

"You're just another one of Zachary's lame attempts to get in our head," Ethan said. "Nothing but a Trojan horse."

As the two knuckleheads barreled past us, Ethan bumped Orlando hard with his shoulder. I could see the anger in Orlando's eyes and noticed him clenching his fists. Me, I was stunned that Danny knew what the term *Trojan horse* meant.

"Come on, man," I said, taking Orlando by the shoulder and turning him back toward his car. "Let's get out of here. I'm tired."

10/MONDAY, NOVEMBER 4—
BUSINESS CLASS & FOOTBALL PRACTICE

When I walked into Coach Whitson's business class on Monday morning, I thought for a brief second that Orlando was back. Sitting in his seat, wearing his Trojans jersey and everything. Except on the back of his jersey, where his name should have been, someone had slapped a strip of tape with *TRAITOR* on it in black Sharpie. It wasn't Orlando at all. It was a dummy, one of the mannequins from the theater department.

The dummy had no lower torso. It was propped up in the chair.

At the front of the room, Shane Hunter sat watching me. He covered his mouth with a hand and tried not to laugh. He failed. Ian and Scott sat behind him. They had their heads down on their desks, also laughing hysterically.

"What do you think of my new art project?" Shane asked. "I've been carrying him around all morning. He's my new best friend."

"I kind of like him," Ian said. "He's a lot quieter than the real Green."

I shook my head, stormed over, and yanked the dummy out of the chair. The other kids in the class, the non-football players, seemed to be enjoying the show.

"So I hear you were out at Wade Jackson's place on Saturday with Orlando," Shane said. "You gonna jump ship and join your BFF on the Raiders now?"

Maybe, I nearly shouted back.

I looked over at Ian. He was our second-string running back. If I *did* ditch the team, he'd be the guy to take my spot. There was hunger in his eyes.

"Look, I just wanted to hang out with my friend," I said. "You remember that concept? Friendship? Because up until a week ago, Orlando was your friend too."

"Well, Orlando sure doesn't look like he needs *me* to be his friend," Shane said. "He can braid hair and have pillow fights with Jack Wayne now."

Ian and Scott snickered like Shane just told the world's greatest joke. The way they blindly followed Shane made me sick.

Maybe being the guy who kept his head down and said nothing wasn't the right tactic to use anymore.

"Yeah, he's made a few friends," I explained. "But it's not perfect over at Athens. Some of the guys on the team, they think he's just one of Coach Z's tricks, like he's just messing with their minds. They call him Z's Trojan horse. So don't act like you know everyth—"

"Shaw, what in the name of God is that?"

Coach Whitson had just entered the room. He was standing behind me with a puzzled expression on his face. It was only then that I realized I was still holding the dummy wearing Orlando's jersey.

"Hunter's idea of a lame joke," I mumbled.

"Devon's hanging out with Green and his Raiders buddies," Shane said.

"Raiders?" Whitson shook his head. "Devon, you need to focus. Concentrate on helping your team win, and stop spending time with that turncoat Orlando. You hear me?"

"Yes, sir," I said quietly.

I handed the doll to Whitson as he walked by. He held it out, read the name on the back, and chuckled. He didn't look mad or disappointed, though. He looked amused.

"All right, sit down," he said. "Shane, see me after class."

"Step it up, ladies!" Coach Colby shouted. "We've only got one game left. Win and we're in the play-offs. Lose and we're the laughingstock of the whole town."

No pressure, huh?

I kicked my knees high and raced up the bleachers alongside the rest of the team. We'd stripped off our shoulder pads and had been running up and down the metal seats of Willard Auto Parts Field for almost five minutes.

This was Coach Z's favorite training measure. For every turnover during a game, we had to run the bleachers for five minutes at Monday's practice. My fumble in the red zone on Friday had been the only Trojan turnover. The second time I'd dropped the ball, the one at the end of the game, the one that nearly cost us a win, didn't count, since I'd fallen on my own fumble. So we only had to run for five minutes instead of ten.

I was at the top of the bleachers when Coach Colby blew his whistle. "That's time!" he shouted. "Bring it in! Hustle! Hustle!" I raced down the bleachers, my cleats ringing metal on metal with each step, my legs feeling like Jell-O, until I'd reached the bottom.

Coach Colby ran practice as we stretched and did sprints. Coach Z stood at the far end of the bleachers with Coach Whitson, talking with a group of men who had been sitting there waiting for us when we walked out of the tunnel. The Friends of Troy. I spied Mr. Willard, Wally Doyle, and Big Bill Norwood—Brian's dad—among them. I couldn't hear what they were saying, but it was pretty clear what they were talking about: Orlando. They'd all seen the paper; they all knew the truth. And the Friends of Troy were chewing Coach Z a new one.

My teammates and I did our usual split, offense taking half of the field, defense the other. By the time we were lining up, Coach Z had rejoined the offense. He looked like someone had taken a dump in his bowl of Wheaties.

"If we want to win, we're going to have to bring our absolute best running game," Coach Z said, folding his thick arms across his chest. "That means no turnovers, complete ball control. You hear me, Shaw?"

"Yes, Coach," I shouted through my mouth guard.

"Let's see it. On the line! Let's go!"

With my wrist bandaged tight—I still hadn't told any of the coaches about how much it actually hurt—I ran hard with each play call. I pushed myself, hitting every hole in the line. I worked until the sun dipped below the horizon. Until the lights of Willard Field were glowing bright, until my breath hitched in my throat and the crisp evening air burned in my lungs.

11/TUESDAY, NOVEMBER 5—
DEVON'S ROOM

I was awake, but I didn't want to get out of bed. I'd barely slept all night, tossing and turning in the sheets. My mind wouldn't shut off.

I'd thought of football and about what my teammates and coaches now thought of me. And then I'd thought about Jack Wayne and his suggestion that I line up behind him in the Raiders backfield.

I could do it. I could play for Athens.

Orlando and I could take the field side by side again. With a supportive team, I could work on getting noticed by recruiters and pick up a full ride to play ball when the time came.

It was decided. I was going to talk to my parents after school today and see what they thought about me transferring over to Athens High.

I propped myself up on my elbows and winced. Every muscle in my body ached from the previous day's practice. My left wrist throbbed. I flexed my fingers and pinpricks of pain stabbed my palm. For the first morning in a long time, I wasn't going to hit the gym. All I'd have been able to do was leg lifts and cardio anyway.

My phone, sitting across my room on my dresser, began to buzz.

Wait, who would be calling me at, like, 6 a.m.?

I groaned and tossed off the covers. A blast of cold air hit me while I staggered across my room, found my phone on top of a stack of fantasy football mags, and checked the screen.

It was Orlando.

I answered. "What's up?" My voice was deeper than normal in that early-morning way.

Orlando didn't say anything.

"Orlando, you there?"

"Hey." He was quiet. Not the Orlando I was used to. Even at six in the morning, I could usually count on him to be the cockiest kid I'd ever met. Something was up. "Can you come over?"

"Dude, we don't go to the same school anymore," I said, trying to lighten his mood. "You need a ride, you're out of luck."

Orlando didn't laugh. "Just swing by, Devon," he said. "Please?"

"Uh, okay."

He hung up before I could say goodbye.

I searched my bedroom floor for clothes that were clean enough to wear to school. Then I shoved my textbooks into my backpack, slung the pack over my shoulder, and headed for the door.

My mom was in the kitchen, brewing a pot of coffee, a whirlwind of energy and activity. "Do you need breakfast?" she asked as she scooped beans into the grinder and gave them a spin.

I shook my head. "Nah, I'm good." I rummaged in the pantry, came up with a couple of energy bars, and hit the road.

Orlando lived not too far from my place, only a couple of miles. The neighborhood he lived in was a little shadier than mine, but it was Troy. Troy wasn't one of those towns that had a wrong side of the tracks. We didn't even really have tracks at all.

When I turned the corner onto Orlando's street, I saw the cop cars right away. One was parked in the driveway, the other on the street, next to Orlando's car. Orlando and his mom stood on the front porch talking to a couple of policemen. His mom was still wearing a white bathrobe and slippers. One of the cops was jotting notes on a small pad of paper.

I pulled up behind Orlando's car and parked. Orlando walked down the driveway to greet me.

"What's going on, man?" I asked. My breath plumed in front of my face. "Why are the cops here?"

"See for yourself." Orlando nodded in the direction of his car. It wasn't fancy or new. It was just a Honda with a ton of miles on it. Orlando's mom had bought it from one of her coworkers.

As I walked around to the driver's side, my questions were answered. The doors and windows had been tagged with red-and-white spray paint. Lines of graffiti zigzagged across the Honda. Someone had sprayed *TROJAN HORSE* on the hood. They'd also sealed the door and hood shut with what must have been industrial-strength white caulk.

"The cops are taking a statement," Orlando said. "Can you give me a couple minutes?"

"Sure thing."

Orlando rejoined his mom and the two cops while I stood next to his car. I leaned in close to examine the caulk, picking at it with one fingernail. It was still a bit spongy, but the cold weather had sped up the drying process. The Honda's door was impossible to open.

Finally, Orlando said his goodbyes and joined me. "So, do you know who did this?" I asked.

"Ain't nobody called me a Trojan horse except those guys on the Raiders' D," Orlando answered. "By the way, I told them you were giving me a ride to school, but there's no way I'm going there today."

"Then where do you want to go?"

He shrugged his shoulders. "Anywhere but here."

"Sure thing, man. Whatever you need."

"Cool. Let's go."

We didn't speak, just listened to the local sports radio anchors drone on about what a great season the Bengals were having and what a (typically) bad season the Browns were having. We drove past Willard Auto Parts, where a string of red-and-white pennants hung from a sign proclaiming *TROY HIGH FOOTBALL FANS GET 1/2 OFF OIL CHANGES.* We passed Doyle's, which wouldn't open until the high school lunch crowd was ready to arrive. Everywhere we drove, the red and white of Troy High were proudly displayed.

"So what are you going to do?" I asked.

"I don't know, man," he said. "I just want to play football."

When I was a couple of blocks from the student parking lot at Troy Central, Orlando said, "Pull over, D."

He popped open the door before the car had come to a stop.

"Where are you going?" I asked.

Orlando shrugged. "Around. I got to think about a few things, you know? Thanks for the lift." He slammed the door shut, rapped his knuckles on the window, and waved.

I pulled away from the curb and continued on toward the parking lot.

In my rearview mirror, I saw Orlando walking away, hands shoved into his coat pockets, hood pulled up to block out the cold. Suddenly, my decision to transfer to Athens didn't seem like the greatest idea anymore.

12/WEDNESDAY, NOVEMBER 6— TROY HIGH SCHOOL & FOOTBALL PRACTICE

I usually drag my chemistry textbook to study hall, but I had left it in my bag early Wednesday morning, distracted by my wrist. After taking Tuesday off, I'd felt guilty and hit the weight room before class. I'd tried to do a few curls, but the pain was still strong. I didn't want to injure the wrist any further, so I eased off on upper-body training and stuck to leg presses. If I hurt myself again, my chances of playing against the Thornton Lions on Friday—or any sort of play-off run we went on after that—would be over.

I dialed in my locker combo, found the hefty textbook, and slammed the door closed.

And that was when I saw them.

Coach Z was walking down the hall toward me. His chest was puffed up with pride. He strode past students and faculty like he owned the place. Walking beside him, wearing his Troy Central High letterman jacket, was Orlando.

Heads turned for the two mighty Trojans. I could hear kids whispering to one another, shocked to see Orlando, the same kids who had booed and cursed his name last week.

I stood there, stunned and unmoving.

"Morning, Shaw," Coach Z said as they passed.

"'Sup, D," Orlando added quietly.

"Uh . . . hi," was all I could muster.

———————————————

Though Orlando was back to being a Trojan, he still hadn't returned to class. The next time

I saw him was in the locker room Wednesday afternoon. I'd practically run from my last class, curious to see if he was going to be at practice and what kind of reception he was going to get from the rest of the team.

Orlando was already suiting up when I got there. A few of the other guys were in the locker room too, including Terry and Ian. Everything looked . . . *normal*. No anger. No raised voices. Just players getting ready to hit the field, like we'd been doing all season long.

"Hey, Devon," Orlando said, offering me a fist bump.

"Sprints in ten minutes!" Coach Whitson called from the far side of the locker room, over by the coaches' office.

I dropped my backpack and shed my school clothes. I wanted to ask Orlando so many things. What happened with his car? Did the Raiders admit to vandalizing it? There was no time, though. And I didn't want to start interrogating him in front of the team.

Orlando could see the questions in my eyes. "The devil you know, am I right?"

I didn't have a response for that.

Orlando tightened his shoulder pads and pulled his jersey over them. The name *TRAITOR* was not taped to the back of this one.

We jogged out of the locker room together, our metal cleats clacking against the cement floor. Coach Whitson was closing the door to the office as we hurried past.

"Welcome back, Green," he said.

Through the tunnel and out onto the field. Side by side. Me and Orlando.

The Friends of Troy were seated in the stands again, the same group of men who had been at Monday's practice. Mr. Willard. Wally Doyle. Big Bill Norwood. They looked infinitely happier today than they had on Monday, though. I wonder why.

I must have been the only person out on the field—including Orlando—who hadn't decided to just press the reset button. Even Shane Hunter seemed happy to see Orlando. After constructing that crude dummy and calling Orlando every name in the book, Shane was smiling and joking around with him.

The reason was clear. With Orlando—our deep threat—sprinting down the sidelines and picking up double coverage by the defense's secondary, the rest of the field opened up for us. The opponent's line became weaker, with more gaps, and we could run the ball more effectively. With the running game established, we could switch it up and run the play-action to Brian. Brian always knew where the first down marker was and could get there before he was tackled.

"Bring it in, everybody!" Coach Z shouted as we completed our sprints. I grabbed my helmet off the bench, jogged to midfield, and took a knee alongside the others. "First things first," Z continued. "You may recognize a familiar face back in our ranks today. Welcome back, Orlando." He smiled. Coach Z, honest to goodness, smiled. The whole team burst into applause.

Orlando waved and said, "Thanks, Coach. So, any of you guys want to help me win a state championship?"

A few of the guys laughed at this, Shane loudest of all.

"Gentlemen, look at those stands over there," Coach Z said. "Friday night, everyone on those bleachers will be here to see *you*. What you've done this season is impressive, but this game and every game from here on out is a must-win situation. So I'm asking you to dig a little deeper, find a little more strength, and persevere. Vince Lombardi said, 'There is only one way to succeed in anything, and that is give it *everything*.' Now . . . line up!"

In unison, the team shouted, "Yes, sir!"

13/FRIDAY, NOVEMBER 8—FINAL HOME GAME AGAINST THE THORNTON LIONS

This was it. Season on the line. If we won, we were in. If we lost, we were done.

The team huddled together in the dark tunnel leading to Willard Field. The air was bitterly cold, colder than any other game we'd played that season. The other Trojans and I slapped each other's shoulder pads, grabbed face masks, and shouted words of encouragement. The tunnel was electric, like our adrenaline had transformed into lightning, crackling and alive.

Coach Z stood in front of us, wearing his lucky sweatshirt and a pair of shorts. Shorts, on a night like this. But football is littered with superstitions, and that was one of Coach Z's. Last home game of the season, no matter the temperature outside, he wore those shorts.

The crowd had started to roar like a jet engine. The band was playing something I couldn't quite make out. The cheerleaders were dancing around midfield, bundled in leg warmers, coats, mittens, and earmuffs. There is infinite truth in the phrase *home-field advantage*.

And then the music stopped. The PA announcer said, "Here they are, your *Troy High TROJANS!*"

"Let's go, troops!" Coach Z bellowed, his voice barely audible over the rumble in the stands. "We've got a battle to win!"

As we ran from the darkness of the tunnel into the glow of the field's sodium floodlights, the band burst into the Troy Central High School fight song. The thousands of fans on the home side of the bleachers began to clap and sing along. The away bleachers, which were actually pretty full considering Thornton was not play-off bound this season, seemed empty compared to the home crowd.

Me, Shane, and Orlando met at midfield with the Lions' QB and halfback for the coin toss. We won the toss and elected to kick off first.

Backed by the crowd's continued cheers, our energy caught Thornton off guard. After a decent runback of the opening kick, the Thornton offense went three and out and were forced to punt.

The punt was high, booming, twisting end over end, getting lost in the lights. The crowd was silent, if only for a moment, before the ball landed in Orlando's hands and he took off down the field. Two defenders pushed him out of bounds just past midfield, starting us inside Lions territory.

I took the first snap, lowering my head and driving forward for about four yards. On a night as cold as that night, each hit was numbingly painful, but the adrenaline pushed me further than I ever thought I could go. My wrist felt better than it had all week, and I held tight to the ball. There was *no way* I was to going to fumble.

My next run, a power option sweep to the left side of the field, gave us a first down and moved the chains. Coach Z's plan was simple. We'd bait the defense into moving up on the line, then surprise them with a pass play from Shane to Orlando across the middle of the field. And it worked perfectly. Twenty yards later, we were already in the red zone. Barely two minutes had ticked off the clock.

Another punishing run up the middle and I chewed up nine yards.

In the huddle, Shane said, "Play action, eighty-eight ghost on one." A fade to the corner of the end zone. He took the snap and faked a hand off to me. The move got Thornton's defense to bite, while Shane floated a perfect pass to Orlando, who was being defended by a single safety. Orlando caught the ball in his fingertips, hauled it in, and slid both of his feet inbounds before falling to the ground.

The ref blew his whistle and threw both

arms into the air. "Touchdown!"

The crowd erupted. Other Trojans swarmed Orlando, slapping him across his pads. Orlando turned to the home bleachers and cupped one hand to the side of his helmet, taking in their adoring cheers.

"It's great to be back!" he shouted to me as we jogged to the sidelines.

Thornton was a decent team, but that night, their plan was simple: they wanted to be spoilers. They didn't have anything to win for, aside from the joy they'd get from keeping us out of the play-offs. And they did an admirable job. Their quarterback marched them down the field, using quick pass plays that caught our defense off guard. When they were down inside the ten-yard line, though, our guys were able to make a stand. Brian Norwood stuffed their running back behind the line of scrimmage on third down. They were forced to kick a field goal.

I ran the ball more in that first half than I ever had before, until I was sweating and heaving and playing with a hitch in my side. It felt like Coach Z was punishing me for considering a move to Athens, even though there was no way for him to know how serious I'd been about the idea.

Late in the second quarter, the score was sixteen to six—Coach Z had gone back to his usual 'two-point conversions only' style of play. We had the ball inside the five, first and goal. I was certain that I was going to get the call, that Z was finally going to let me break the goal line and score a TD.

Shane crouched into the huddle. "Twenty-one wildcat," he said.

A halfback pass play. I could try to run the ball in. Or if the defense pounced on the run, I could pass the ball off to a wide receiver or a tight end. It was a trick play, something Coach Z didn't do very often.

We lined up. The crowd matched our intensity—they were so loud I could barely hear Shane calling out the signals. When our center hiked the ball, Shane dropped back, turned, and laid the ball right in my stomach. I took two steps forward, head down like I was going to barrel through the line. The Lions bit. Their secondary rushed forward, collapsing into the line and leaving the middle of the field wide open.

Which is exactly where Orlando stood.

I stepped back and lobbed the ball over the line, into his waiting arms.

He strolled into the end zone untouched.

The score at the half was twenty-four to six, and we never looked back. During the second half, we mostly ran the ball in order to eat up the clock and maximize our time of possession. The deeper into the game we went, the more my wrist—my whole *body*—ached. But I did my job, went out there, and found any seam I could.

But the night belonged to Orlando. Coach Z was proud to have him back on the field, and he showed his prize player to the crowd every chance he could.

Late in the game, we were up by three touchdowns, with the ball at the fifty-yard line. Coach called for the corner route, the same play that started the Orlando-in-Athens fiasco.

Shane dropped back to pass. I stepped up to block on the right side of the line and dropped a blitzing linebacker to his knees. I heard Shane grunt behind me, knew the ball was in the air, and craned my neck to watch downfield. I was completely exposed—a defender could have easily flattened me. Thankfully, none did.

The ball was a laser beam, blasting through double coverage and sailing right into Orlando's hands. He sprinted in for his third touchdown reception of the night.

The crowd loved every second of it.

I hoped Jack Wayne and all of the jerks over at Athens, especially the ones who vandalized Orlando's car, would see the game highlights. I hoped they saw, and I hoped they were scared. Because we were gunning for them.

When the final buzzer sounded and the cannons outside the field boomed and echoed through the crisp Troy night, we had won by a score of forty to thirteen.

The team, the stands, the band, the cheerleaders, the parents, the Friends of Troy, they all mobbed the field. I found myself in the middle of the melee, surrounded by teammates who were hoisting one another into the air. I saw

Orlando and bounced my way past other players until I reached him.

He tore off his helmet and wrapped his arms around me in a wicked bear hug. He lifted me into the air and shouted, "Play-offs, here we come! Yeah, baby!"

14/FRIDAY, NOVEMBER 8—
THE TROY LOCKER ROOM

Our celebration continued in the locker room, where someone—I think it was Brian Norwood—started singing the Troy High fight song. Soon enough, we'd all joined in. The cement walls of the locker room reverberated with our voices.

I'd never felt this amazing in my life.

As I stood by my locker, stripping off the sweaty black shirt I wore under my uniform, I saw the Friends of Troy stride into the room. Mr. Willard had a big smile on his face. He went around shaking everyone's hand and congratulating each one of us on a game well played.

"Way to continue the winning tradition here at Troy, son," he said to Shane Hunter, clasping QB1's hand.

Big Bill Norwood hugged Brian, and Wally Doyle extended his arms and shouted, "The restaurant is all yours tonight, boys! Come and enjoy some celebratory pizzas!" I knew there would be a party elsewhere too, where more . . . exciting things than pizza would be served. But we'd start at Doyle's, and that was all right.

It was going to be a long night.

Coach Z stood behind everyone, a smile stretched across his face.

I took my time showering and dressing. The rest of the guys were eager to hit Doyle's, which would be crawling with cheerleaders and other girls from our class, so they sprayed themselves with too much deodorant or cologne and headed on their way.

Orlando smacked me on the head as he

passed by. "Hey, man, my car is still out of action," he said. "You mind if I snag a ride?"

"Yeah, sure."

"Cool. Meet you outside."

I finished dressing, gathered my things, and slammed my locker closed. As I walked past the coaches' office, I glanced through the slats in the window. Coach Whitson and Shane sat inside, talking. They hadn't noticed me, but I could hear them just fine.

"Thanks again, Shane," Whitson said. "And thank Ian and Scott for us too."

"Sure thing, Coach," Shane said.

"Great game out there."

I ducked behind a row of lockers as they exited the office. Coach Whitson left the door ajar.

When both Whitson and Shane had gone down the hall leading out to the parking lot, I stepped to the office door and peered inside. I don't know what I thought I'd find. Probably nothing. I shook my head, was about to turn and walk away, when something under Coach Whitson's metal desk caught my attention: a white plastic bag from a local hardware store.

I couldn't be sure of the bag's contents. But I could have sworn I saw the bulges of two or three cans of spray paint.

Nah. That can't be right. I'm seeing things.

I wanted to get a closer look, though, because right then, I was starting to think that Shane Hunter and some of the other guys were responsible for vandalizing Orlando's car, not his Athens teammates. And under Coach Whitson's—maybe even Coach Z's—orders. And that was just stupid.

Wasn't it?

I hesitated. Did I really want to know the truth? What if it meant losing Orlando for good? We were two games away from a state championship—from Troy High School immortality. And wasn't that the dream?

"Hey! Anybody left in here?" Coach Whitson's voice scared the crap out of me. I jumped back from the open door like it was scorching hot and prayed Whitson didn't see me snooping.

"Yeah," I answered. "Coming, Coach!"

Coach Whitson rounded the corner from

the hall leading outside. "Get the lead out, Shaw," he said. "You've got celebrating to do, right?"

"Right, Coach." I opened my mouth, almost spoke up about the plastic bag. But instead, I added, "Great to have Orlando back, isn't it?"

"Darn straight," Coach Whitson said with a smile. "They better clear a nice big spot in the school's trophy case, because that state championship is ours for the taking."

I smiled back. "Agreed."

"Now, get out of here. Go get yourself some pizza, and have a little fun. But not too much fun, all right?"

"Yes, sir," I said, lowering my head, moving to the exit, and doing what the coach asked me to do.

ABOUT THE AUTHOR

Brandon Terrell is the author of numerous books for young readers, including picture books, novels, and graphic novels. He is also one of the writers for *The Choo Choo Bob Show*, an educational children's television program about trains. When not hunched over his laptop, Brandon enjoys watching movies and television, reading, baseball, and spending every spare moment with his wife and their two children.

WINNING IS *NOT OPTIONAL.*

OUT of THE TUNNEL

BREAKTHROUGH

THE OPTION

AT ALL COSTS

TAKE AWAY

RISE ABOVE

WELCOME TO

THE DOJO

BODY SHOT

SIDE CONTROL

LEARN TO FIGHT,
LEARN TO LIVE,
AND LEARN
TO FIGHT
FOR YOUR
LIFE.

HEAD KICK

TRIANGLE CHOKE

THE CATCH

TRAVEL TEAM
FORCED OUT

TRAVEL TEAM
HIGH HEAT

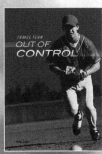

TRAVEL TEAM
OUT OF CONTROL

TRAVEL TEAM
POWER HITTER

TRAVEL TEAM
THE PROSPECT

LOOK FOR THESE TITLES FROM THE

TRAVEL TEAM

COLLECTION.